Sleepy Bear

Written and Cover Designed by Nadia Garnier
Illustrations by Tanya Ramsey

This Little Red Diamond Book Belongs To:

This book is dedicated to

The **Mitchell-Garnier** Family

without whom my dreams would not be possible

~*~*~*~

Special Thanks to the very first backers of this effort:

Pamela Palmer, Abigail DeHaan, Lisa Garnier, Janaye Bryant, Joanna Wiszniewska, Judy Patno, Noelle Patno, George Robins, April Watkins, Corey Knapke, Angela Allen, and Mel Jordan Jett

RedDiamondLit.com

Sleepy Bear

Copyright © 2013 by Red Diamond Literary

Written and Cover Designed by Nadia Garnier
Illustrations by Tanya Ramsey

First Edition

Published in The United States.

First Printed: May 2014

ISBN 978-0-9913250-1-6
Library of Congress Control Number: 2014908007

Editors: Lisa Garnier, Elane Merari, Noelle Patno, Brenna Pepper, and Esther Whitlock

For more information on Red Diamond Literary publications, go to: **RedDiamondLit.com**

Far Far away, in the land of Hush and Slumber,
Lived a village of Whatzits, far too many to number.

They worked and they played and cared for each other,
And when in need, they shared with one another.

The curious thing about this village, which made it such a lovely place to be,
Was that every child could have their own Living Teddy Bear. Some children had 2 or 3.

Living Teddy Bears made wonderful friends. They helped the children with whatever they might need. So it was with that Joy that a little bear named, *Sleepy,* by a girl named *Marisol* was received.

It was *Marisol's* 7th birthday, a spectacular day of fun,
For every birthday in Hush and Slumber was celebrated by everyone,

Papa planned out the day for *Marisol* and her friends, down to the last detail,
Rides at the fair, racing go-carts, and a big show at the circus would prevail.

As fantastic as the plans were, *Marisol* was worried about one small wish-list item. She longed and longed for her own living bear, she was the only kid in town without one.

But she feared Papa had forgotten, he worked very hard all the time you see.
He worked twice as hard because *Marisol's* Mama had gone to heaven when she was a baby.

So Marisol did her chores and never complained, for Papa was such a wonderful Papa; honest and kind,
And she knew Living Bears took years to hatch and at least 3 days journey to find.

She always made sure to clean up her room, and to help with supper, but she hoped and she prayed,
And she wished and wished that she'd have a little furry friend to love and play with someday.

So the big day came and the whole town brought presents, 172 in all; there were 28 birthdays that day!
Marisol was happy to receive 6 small boxes, given to her by her friends joyfully.

A bright pink scarf, and pale blue galoshes, an orange jump rope, and a box full of purple knicker knacks,
A fancy set of 7 teacups, and one tiny box came last.

The last box was from Papa, and all it contained was a small handwritten note, tied with a bow.

It said, "To my dearest Marisol, I hope you enjoy this gift I give with love. He took 7 years to hatch and grow."

Marisol looked up at Papa who was smiling from ear to ear.

He had just produced something, that was hidden behind his back, which made all her friends laugh and cheer.

"A Living Bear! Papa, Oh thank you so much! It was all I wanted in this whole entire world!"

Marisol hugged Papa tight and kissed her new bear, as Papa said smiling, "Anything for my little girl."
"His name is Sleepy, and he comes from the rarest of all the living bears,
A Polar, Ursus maritimus, you can tell by his snow white fur, dear."

"There are only a few left of his kind,
So please love him well and take great care.
Before you were born, Mama made a 10 days journey to find him,
To give you a most special bear.

She planted his egg under a lavender bush.
I've tended and watered him all this time.
So you see, Sleepy is a gift that is truly hers and truly mine."

"Oh thank you Papa, I promise to always love him," said *Marisol*, as she hugged *Sleepy* bear, And he hugged her back.

She kissed Papa goodbye as she ran off to play with all her friends and their bears,
As they got in line at the first roller coaster track.

"Tell us all about yourself!" Said Marisol's friend Kelsey to the new bear,
With her panda Pom sitting at her shoulders, braiding up her long dark hair,

"Well, I'm called *Sleepy*", said the bear, "I'm not sure why, but that's what I'm told.
I can leap over a whole house, and fight off a lion... well, I think I could...maybe when I'm 8 years old."

All the children laughed, as *Sleepy* blushed at his own silly boasting ways.
"It's time for fun and games!" said Eldon's grizzly Zolton. "Let's not waste the day!"

They took *Sleepy* to a baseball game, he was very excited to be there,
But he fell asleep in his popcorn, even with the crowds loud cheers.

They went go-cart racing, but *Sleepy* didn't drive very far,
After only one short lap, he began to nap in the car.

Marisol said, "I know what will keep you awake, there's lots of excitement at circus shows!"

But, before the elephants had even walked the tight rope, *Sleepy* slipped under the benches for a doze.

Then Marisol decided to take Sleepy home for some tea.
She scooped him up and whispered, "It's been a pretty long day, hasn't it, for you and me?"

At bedtime, *Sleepy* nodded and smiled shyly, "I'm sorry if I wasn't much fun today."
Then *Marisol* looked at him with surprise, "Don't say that; you were great in every way."

"No one else was able to balance all the bottles at the fair.
But, you did it in one try. You are a very impressive bear."

"But, Sleepy, please tell me, why are you always so tired?"
He looked at her with big round eyes and said, "I don't know."

"I just get so warm and happy inside, you love me so well that my heart fills with joy,
And I drift away wherever I go."

"And I dream of dancing clouds and rainbows jumping over the sea.
It's because I'm so very happy, from all the care you give to me."

Marisol cuddled *Sleepy* up into her arms and hugged him tight, tight, tight.
"I never had such a friend as you, my *Sleepy* bear. I will love you always. Sleep well tonight."

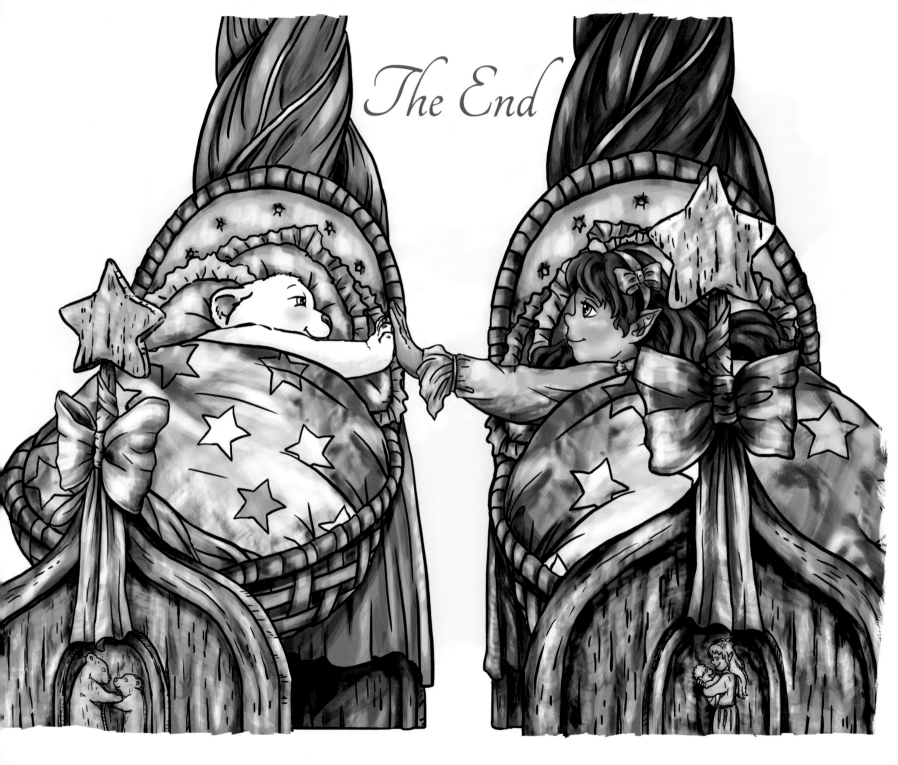

The End

About the Author
Nadia Garnier

Nadia Garnier was born in 1980 in the eclectic suburb of Takoma Park, Maryland. Her writing career began at the age of 9 with her first children's book "The Little Mermaid," an adventure story of a young mermaid and her sea creature friends, created through a school writing program. Raised happily with her four older siblings by parents of St. Lucian and Guyanese descent, she developed a flair for depicting themes of small island ideals and family values in her writing. Nadia continued to write and to collect her stories without an outlet, until she founded her own independent production company, Red Diamond Films, Inc. in 2003. Once she completed her bachelor's degree in Behavior, Ecology, Evolution, and Systematics in the biological sciences, she was able to shift her focus. She began to use her film production company as a vehicle for the many stories she had written over the years.

In 2004, Nadia made her first short film and published a book of poetry and artwork entitled, "My Soul On Paper." By 2007, she had written, produced and directed six short films. All of her short films have successfully garnered attention. Her debut short film, "Fanatic," received three official selections at foreign film festivals. Her animated short, "New Numa," won 14th place; a monetary prize, surpassing hundreds of competing entries in a youtube.com short competition. Ouat Media, Inc. began distributing three of her short films after a successful pitch at the Cannes Film Festival in 2008. Finally, her most recent film, an action-packed horror/thriller about a mysterious late night attacker at a local laundromat entitled "Washing," is currently touring the film festival circuit.

Nadia has now lived in California for the past five years. While taking a break between making short films and launching the campaign to fund her first feature film, she is currently working on transforming some of her favorite short stories into children's books. In 2013, she launched the publishing arm of Red Diamond Films, Inc., Red Diamond Literary, in order to share the stories closest to her heart with children of all ages. Slated to be released in 2014, her next two titles are currently in production: 1) "The Littlest Light," a story about the bravery of a small glowing light who risks it all to save a friend, and 2) "One Night in the Land of Nod," a tale of a mischievous little boy who happens upon a secret gathering of fairies only to find that he is the guest of honor. Find out more at NadiaGarnier.com

About the Illustrator
Tanya Ramsey

Tanya J Ramsey has been in the field of graphic design for over 10 years. Her passion has always been in creature design; whether drawing realistic animals, delightful cartoons, or creatures of fantasy. In 2004, she left her birth state of Minnesota in order to pursue art opportunities in Anchorage, Alaska. Starting out at a retail art store, Tanya quickly found clients eager to hire her for a variety of illustration projects including; book illustration, courtroom drawing, and wall murals. Several years later, she broke into the field of graphic design.

Tanya spent the next 7 years working as a graphic artist for a number of employers. However, her home state was calling her name. So, in the Fall of 2012, Tanya moved back home to Minnesota to begin her career as a full time freelance illustrator.

Tanya is proficient with a wide variety of traditional media such as pen & ink, graphite, scratch board, and marker. In the last 10 years, she has also developed her abilities with digital illustration using Photoshop and Illustrator. Find out more at tjr-cool-graphics.com